Prep Gr

FINNEY CO. PUBLIC LIBRARY
605 E. WALNUT
GARDEN CITY, KS 67846

P9-DCZ-344

THE WORLD FAMOUS
TULLMAN
CIRCUS

MUNICIPAL AUDITORIUM
TICKETS $5.00

the chocolate chip cookie contest

story by barbara douglass

pictures by eric jon nones

J 83223
Prep.

lothrop, lee & shepard books
new york

Text copyright © 1985 by Barbara Douglass. Illustrations © 1985 by Eric Jon Nones. All rights reserved. No part of this book may be reproduced or utilized in any form or by any means, electronic or mechanical, including photocopying, recording or by any information storage and retrieval system, without permission in writing from the Publisher. Inquiries should be addressed to Lothrop, Lee & Shepard Books, a division of William Morrow & Company, Inc., 105 Madison Avenue, New York, New York 10016. Printed in the United States of America. First Edition. 1 2 3 4 5 6 7 8 9 10

Library of Congress Cataloging in Publication Data. Douglass, Barbara, (date). The chocolate chip cookie contest. Summary: A small boy learns to bake chocolate chip cookies with a difference, and wins first prize in a cookie contest. [1. Cookies—Fiction. 2. Baking—Fiction. 3. Contests—Fiction] I. Nones, Eric Jon, ill. II. Title. PZ7.D7479Ch 1985 [E] 84-5682 ISBN 0-688-04043-8 ISBN 0-688-04044-6 (lib. bdg.)

This one is for Patrick and Gregory,
our two new Douglasses,
for Dorothy,
who inspired and tested the recipe,
and for Sharon—
B.D.

To all my family,
with love—
E.J.N.

"Hey, Cory! Listen to this!" shouted my friend Kevin. "There's a chocolate chip cookie contest at the shopping center. I'm going to make some and win two tickets to the circus!"

"Do you know how to make cookies?" I asked.

"Sure," said Kevin. "I've watched my mom. All you do is mix up some flour and stuff and bake it in the oven until it's cookies."

"I can't use the stove unless a grown-up helps," I told him.

"That's the problem," said Kevin. "Mom's busy painting right now and I have to hurry. The judges start tasting cookies and choosing winners today at four o'clock."

"I'd rather be a cookie taster," I told him, "than a cookie baker."

Kevin grabbed my arm. "Ask your baby-sitter to help," he said, dragging me inside. "She makes the best chocolate chip cookies ever."

Mrs. Anderson was chasing the twins and the twins were chasing the cat. "Bake cookies? Here? Today?" she asked. "No way! Try me next week."

"Next week will be too late," we told her. So she gave us her special recipe.

"Promise to look both ways crossing the street, Cory, and go ask your grandmother to help. She makes cookies almost as good as mine."

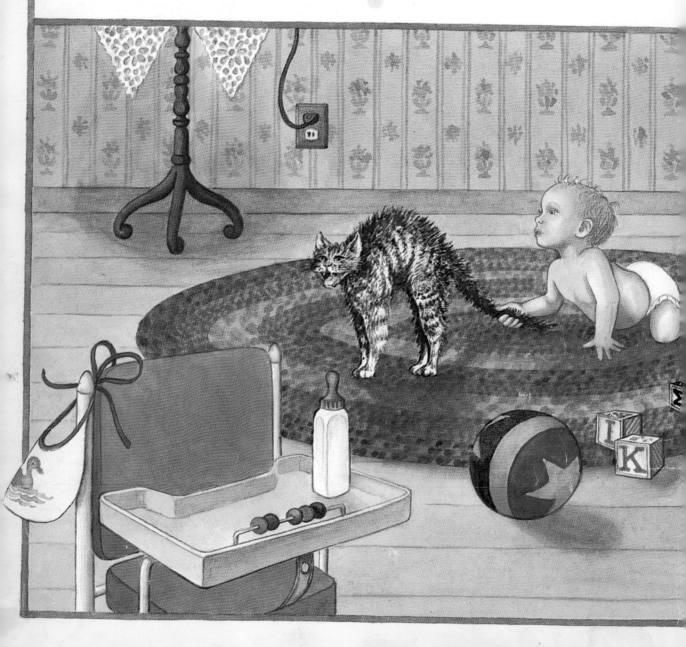

My grandmother was just leaving. "Mercy me!" she exclaimed when she checked the recipe. "You can't make prize-winning cookies this way. You'll need to add one-half cup of these." She gave us a box of raisins. "Now go see if your Aunt Suzanne can help. She makes cookies almost as good as mine."

Aunt Suzanne was eating a late lunch. She still had three chimneys to clean before dark. "Good grief," she groaned when she checked the recipe. "You can't make prize-winning cookies this way. You'll need to add one-half cup of these." She gave us a package of walnuts. "Now go see if Cousin Norman can help. He makes cookies almost as good as mine."

Cousin Norman was picking his banjo. "Great guns!" he boomed when he checked the recipe. "You can't make prize-winning cookies this way. You'll need to add one-half cup of this." He gave us a package of coconut. "Now go try next door. Mrs. Luigi makes cookies almost as good as mine."

Mrs. Luigi was right in the middle of plum jam and piccalilli relish. She wiped her hands and checked the recipe. "This ought to be a prize-winner, all right." Then she gave us a big package of chocolate chips. "I see my son Larry in his backyard now. Run outside and see if he can help. Watch out, though, he's no cookie expert."

"I have to get changed," said Larry Luigi, "so you'll be on your own."

"That's okay," I told him. "Kevin knows what to do."

"Let me get my things from the trailer," said Larry. "I must be at the shopping center by four o'clock."

"We'll work fast," I told him. "That's when we have to be there, too."

"All right," said Larry. "Promise to clean up your own mess and it's a deal. I can even give you a ride."

I had to ask Mrs. Anderson about that. Kevin called his mom, too, while Larry put sugar and flour and eggs and bowls and beaters and things on the counter.

Our hands weren't very dirty, but Larry made us wash them anyway. He had everything else we needed for the recipe except the cookie sheets. So he brought out two pizza pans instead. Then he turned on the oven.

"Call me if you need anything else," he said, "and watch the clock. It's already after two."

There was more to it than just mixing up some stuff in a bowl. The first thing Kevin read was "grease cookie sheets."

"What does that mean?" I asked him. Kevin didn't know, so I yelled for Larry.

Larry showed us how to spread just a little bit of butter all over the pans so the cookies wouldn't stick. Then he hurried back to his room.

Kevin read from the recipe, "Cream butter, peanut butter and sugars." I yelled for Larry again.

In a few minutes Larry came out and showed us how to smoosh the butter and peanut butter together. Then he said to add the sugars and stir hard until the mixture was creamy smooth.

FINNEY CO. PUBLIC LIBRARY
GARDEN CITY, KS 67846

Kevin said, "Cory, you can stir. I'll watch and tell you when it's ready."

I stirred and I stirred and I stirred. I thought my arm would fall off before Kevin said the stuff was creamy enough. Then he read from the recipe again.

FINNEY CO. PUBLIC LIBRARY
605 E. WALNUT
GARDEN CITY, KS 67846

I had to call Larry three more times.
First, he showed us how to beat the eggs.
Next, he showed us how to sift the flour.
Last, he showed us how to blend it in. Then he said, "Think you can handle the rest of this? If I don't finish my face soon we're all going to be late."

I dumped in the oatmeal, Grandma's raisins and Aunt Suzanne's walnuts and what was left of Mrs. Luigi's chocolate chips.

Kevin stared at the bowl and said, "Looks like you made too much dough, Cory."

"So give me half," I told him. "Maybe I can win a prize too."

"You don't have time," Kevin insisted. "You still have to clean up the mess."

I had plenty of time. It only took a minute or so to spread out my dough on one of the pans.

When Kevin's pan was ready too, I called Larry again. He put everything in the oven and set the timer. I washed bowls and beaters and things while Kevin sat and stared at his Mickey Mouse watch. "Just in case the timer doesn't work," he said. "We have to be sure the cookies don't burn."

When Kevin's cookies were done I noticed Cousin Norman's coconut. "Larry!" I cried.

It was too late to add it to Kevin's cookies, so I said, "Just let me dump it on top of mine, please. I can't make prize-winning cookies without coconut."

"You won't win the prize anyway," said Kevin on the way to the shopping center. "That looks more like a monster cookie than a people cookie."

I wondered if Kevin was right.

"It's supposed to look like that," Larry told him. "Cory's a pizza man, like me."

"Yeah," I added. "Don't you know a chocolate chip pizza cookie when you see one?"

"Oh, boy, is that dumb!" said Kevin. "The judges are all going to laugh. They're all going to say they never heard of such a thing, and I'm going to win the prize."

"Maybe you will," I told him. "And maybe you won't."

The judges tasted lots and lots of cookies before they got to mine.

And Kevin was right.

They did laugh.

They did say they never had heard of such a thing as a chocolate chip pizza cookie.

But I didn't care . . . because . . .

CORY'S PRIZE-WINNING CHOCOLATE CHIP COOKIE

INGREDIENTS

2 sticks (1 cup) butter or margarine (let soften at room temperature
   for an hour or two before you begin mixing, to make creaming easier)
½ cup peanut butter, smooth or chunky
1 cup brown sugar (packed)
½ cup white sugar
2 eggs
2 cups flour
1 teaspoon baking soda
1½ cups oatmeal, quick-cooking or old-fashioned
½ cup chopped walnuts
½ cup raisins
6 ounces chocolate chips (1 small bag or ½ large bag)
½ cup coconut flakes

UTENSILS

1 large pizza pan or 1 large cookie sheet, measuring 14½ inches across
1 large mixing bowl
2 medium bowls
   egg beater or fork
   flour sifter
   measuring cups and spoons
   large mixing spoon

First, assemble all ingredients and utensils, then wash your hands
(even if they're not dirty). Grease pizza pan or cookie sheet and set
aside. Preheat oven to 375 degrees. You may need a grown-up's help
with this

Cream butter, peanut butter, and sugars in large bowl. Stir until well mixed and smooth.

Break two eggs into medium bowl and beat until foamy, using egg beater or fork. Pour into large bowl and use spoon to blend beaten eggs into creamy mixture.

Sift flour and baking soda into second medium bowl. Add half to dough and stir gently. Then add the rest, and blend well.

Add oatmeal and stir gently until well mixed. Add walnuts, raisins, and chocolate chips, again stirring gently.

Use mixing spoon to scrape dough from bowl onto pizza pan. Pat out dough with clean hands until it evenly covers entire pan. (If using cookie sheet, spread dough into circle about 14½ inches across and ½ inch deep.)

Bake for 10 minutes. Remove from oven and sprinkle coconut on top of dough, patting it down with back of spoon. Continue baking for another 15 minutes (wash bowls and beaters and things while you wait), or until the cookie is firm and golden brown.

Allow cookie to cool slightly, slice pizza-style.

To make Kevin's cookies, drop dough by heaping teaspoons onto greased cookie sheet. Bake 10 minutes or until golden brown.

Recipe makes one cookie pizza or about five dozen drop cookies.